This book belongs to:

This book is dedicated to
my mother who read to me.
She gave me a lifelong love
of reading and books.

# Where Did All The Animals Go?

## The Cowboy Dog Series

Written by Mary Stern  Illustrated by Kathy Ann Sullivan

"Nicholas, let's go for a hike."

"I think you will like the birds and the bees
the flowers and the trees."

At the start of the trail,
the magpie flaps her tail
and caws to the crow,
"You must warn the doe!"

The crow flies off and cries out to the doe, "Hikers are near. Stay in the trees, lie low."

The doe walks in the woods
and sees the raccoon.
"Stay away from the trail.
They'll be here soon."

The raccoon looks over and tells the bear,
"There's a little boy coming.
Stay in your lair."

The bear spots
the mountain lion
up in a tree.

"Don't come down.
It's no time to run free."

The cougar peers down and says to the mole,
"Watch out. Get back down in your hole."

The mole peeks out and spies the snake on the path. "You better slither off. Forget your sunbath."

The snake sees the skunk getting a drink.
"You should go hide. Don't make a stink."

The magpie and crow
follow them back to the car.
"The forest is ours again
– at least so far."

"The forest and the trees,"

"The birds and the bees,"

"The magpie and the crow,"

Special thanks to my husband for his support; to Elizabeth and Jeremy for their assistance; to Reuben for providing all of his technical expertise; to Nicholas for being my special hiking pal.

Book Design by Jeremy Hageman

Library of Congress Cataloging – in Publication Data

Stern, Mary
Where Did All of the Animals Go? by Mary Stern; illustrated by Kathy Ann Sullivan

Printed and bound in the USA

http://www.cowboydogseries.com

Nicholas is a five year old cowboy who lives in rural Kansas. He loves all of his farm animals and kindergarten.

Tawny is a six year old Mountain Cur. She lives in Colorado Springs with her humans and loves hiking.